# BAND GEEKS
## Shredding with the Geeks

Calico

An Imprint of Magic Wagon
www.abdopublishing.com

by Amy Cobb
Illustrated by Anna Cattish

For Hope James, my most loyal canine friend. —AC

**www.abdopublishing.com**

Published by Magic Wagon, a division of ABDO,
PO Box 398166, Minneapolis, Minnesota 55439.
Copyright © 2015 by Abdo Consulting Group, Inc.

Printed in the United States of America, North Mankato, Minnesota.
102014
012015

THIS BOOK CONTAINS
RECYCLED MATERIALS

Written by Amy Cobb
Illustrations by Anna Cattish
Edited by Heidi M.D. Elston, Megan M. Gunderson & Bridget O'Brien
Cover and interior design by Candice Keimig
Extra special thanks to David Manthei, our snowboarding expert

**Library of Congress Cataloging-in-Publication Data**

Cobb, Amy, author.
  Shredding with the geeks / by Amy Cobb ; illustrated by Anna Cattish.
    pages cm. -- (Band geeks)
  Summary: When her grandparents sign her up for the Benton Bluff
Junior High band Tally Nguyen is horrified and worried about what the
kids on her snowboarding team will think--but she comes to realize that
she doesn't need to choose between the groups.
  ISBN 978-1-62402-076-6
  1. Bands (Music)--Juvenile fiction. 2.  Vietnamese American children-
-Juvenile fiction. 3.  Snowboarding--Juvenile fiction. 4.  Grandparent
and child--Juvenile fiction. 5.  Junior high schools--Juvenile fiction.
[1. Bands (Music)--Fiction. 2. Vietnamese Americans--Fiction. 3.
Snowboarding--Fiction. 4. Grandparents--Fiction. 5. Junior high
schools--Fiction. 6. Schools--Fiction.]  I. Cattish, Anna, illustrator. II.
Title.
  PZ7.1.C63Sh 2015
  813.6--dc23
                              2014033608

With extra special thanks to Larry Vaught for graciously
sharing his expertise and passion for music.
I am forever grateful to Clelia Gore, Megan Gunderson,
and Candice Keimig for taking a chance on me. —AC

# TABLE OF CONTENTS

# Chapter 1
## BRAND NEW BAND GEEK

**Extreme. That's me. Mainly because of** slopestyle snowboarding. That's my sport. No, it's my life. But there's something else extreme in my life. My grandparents. No joke. I never know what they'll do next. And when I got home from school, they struck again.

"Tally, check out your grandparents," my friend Yulia Glatt said. Yulia goes to the same school as me, Benton Bluff Junior High. And her house is across the street from mine. We moved here five years ago when I was in second grade. So Yulia is pretty much used to my grandparents by now. Or as used to them as anyone could get, anyhow.

My grandparents emigrated from Vietnam a long time ago, right after they got married. But they still want to try everything this country has to offer. And I mean *everything*.

Today, it was ballroom dancing. They twirled in front of our huge family room picture window, totally visible from the street. Grammy wore a fluffy, red feather boa. Pop's fancy rhinestone shirt sparkled in the setting sun as he spun her around.

"I gotta go, Yulia," I said. "Time to close the blinds before the entire block sees them."

"I think they're cute." Yulia smiled.

"Cute? That's because you don't live with them."

"True," she said. "Have fun."

"Wanna help? I'll probably need backup."

"Sorry." Yulia held up her clarinet case. "Mr. Byrd gave us new music to play at the Snow Ball."

How could I forget? It was our first week back to school after winter break. And the annual winter dance was coming up soon.

"I'm guessing we couldn't get a real band this year? So we're stuck with the Band O' Geeks instead?" The Band O' Geeks is what I call our school band. Playing clarinet in the band is Yulia's life, just like snowboarding is mine. But I don't get band. I mean, sitting around blowing hot air into an instrument? Snooze fest!

"We *are* a real band. And we're playing a love song." Yulia wiggled her eyebrows up and down. "And hey," she laughed, "watch it with that geek stuff."

"Sorry." I laughed, too. "But you know I'm not talking about you, Yulia. You're a cool geek. I meant the rest of the Band O' Geeks."

Yulia shook her head. "At least we're not a bunch of park rats!" She teases me about snowboarding as much as I tease her about band.

"Whatever, band girl. Go practice your new song."

"And you go practice, uh, whatever park rats practice."

"Later!" I said, jumping up and grabbing a pretend snowboard. Yulia laughed as she left.

When I opened the front door, it sounded like a live band was playing inside. I plugged my ears all the way to the family room where my grandparents were still dancing.

"The entire neighborhood can see you, you know!" I shouted above the music.

"Let them see. I don't care." Pop twirled Grammy around a few times before dipping her.

Grammy giggled and slapped Pop's shoulder. "Let me up, Quan."

He did. And then he kissed her cheek.

"Silly man," Grammy said. But I knew she loved it. And she loved him. It showed in her sparkly, brown eyes. And in the way she tickled his cheek with her boa.

"So what's for supper?" I asked, turning the music off and heading toward the kitchen. "I smell *chè bắp*!"

Grammy still cooks a lot of Vietnamese foods, and *chè bắp* is sweet corn pudding. Yummy! I couldn't resist dipping my finger into the bowl before Grammy swiped it away.

"Uh, uh, uh!" Grammy's voice rose higher with every "uh."

"What?" I asked, licking the sticky pudding from my finger.

"That's for dessert. Please use your manners, Tally."

I grinned. "Taste testing is good manners, Grammy. And your *chè bắp* is officially the best!"

She tried to frown, but her lips curved into a smile instead. "Supper will be ready soon. We're having *cá kho tộ* tonight."

Mmm. Fish simmered in caramel sauce and spices in Grammy's clay pot. It's one of my favorites. I rubbed my stomach. "Good! I'm starving," I said. "And I need my energy for snowboarding practice."

Grammy patted my shoulder. "Your grandfather and I want to talk to you about that." She pulled out a stool. "Sit."

I hopped onto the stool. But I didn't like the serious look on Grammy's face. "What's up? If it's about dipping into the pudding, I promise I'll never do it again. Until the next time you make *chè bắp*," I tried to joke.

"It's not that," Pop said, joining us in the kitchen.

"Is it my grades? Because I've kept them up. No way will I get kicked off the snowboarding team."

Grammy shook her head. "No, Tally. We're really proud of your first semester grades." She paused. "But it is about snowboarding."

Okay, now I was super nervous. When I first mentioned snowboarding a few years ago, I had to beg my grandparents to let me try it. For one thing, the drive to practice takes an hour. For another, they were afraid I'd get hurt. But so far, I hadn't.

"I'm not dropping the snowboarding team, if that's what this is about." I crossed my arms. "Forget it. Not happening!"

"No," Pop said. "We're not asking you to drop the team. But we want you to develop more interests."

Grammy nodded. "Snowboarding is fun. For now. But it isn't something you can do forever."

"It is, too," I argued.

"How many grandmas are snowboarders?"

She had me there. "I'm sure there are some! I can teach you! Do you want to learn how to ollie? Or maybe nail the rails?"

"Neither." Grammy leaned against the counter. "And I'm serious, Tally. Everyone needs life skills."

*Nooooo. Not life skills again.* Last month, Grammy signed me up for a candlemaking class. Before that, it was a coupon clipping workshop. Why? I don't have enough cash to even worry about saving money yet. Besides, most coupons are for products for cats or bladder problems. So far, I didn't have either of those.

"Life skills are for people who can't snowboard," I finally said.

"Snowboarders need life skills, too," Pop said. "That's why we talked to Mr. Byrd."

"Whoa! The band director at my school? Why?"

"Of course, the one at your school, silly. You're all signed up for band." Now Grammy tried to tickle my cheek with her boa. But I hopped off the stool, dodging it.

"Congratulations, Tally! You're playing French horn, and your first practice is tomorrow," Pop said.

Suddenly Gabe Creek popped into my brain. Gabe used to be on the snowboarding team, and he played in band. So the team nicknamed him Creek the Band Geek because he totally lost focus on snowboarding. But then the army stationed his mom somewhere else, so his family moved this fall.

No way was I going to be picked on for being the new Creek the Band Geek. My last name didn't even rhyme with geek. Nguyen the Band Geek? No. Plus, Grammy and Pop forgot one little thing.

"I don't even have a French horn. I have an electric guitar, remember?" I said.

Guitar lessons was another life skill they'd signed me up for a few years ago. At first, reading the music was too hard. But when I learned to play mostly by ear, I really got into it. Until I started snowboarding. Then my guitar sort of got shoved to the back of the closet behind my gear.

I still drag it out now and then. But very few people know I play guitar. Not even the snowboarding team. Not like guitar is uncool or anything. But it's hard enough to be even a little bit cool, and snowboarding is my way in. But my grandparents don't make it easy. They're happy being completely un-normal. And now band!

"Of course I remember. But there aren't any guitarists in the school band," Grammy said. "Mr. Byrd is giving you a school-loaner French horn."

"Ew! I don't want an instrument still oozing leftover kid spit." I stuck out my tongue, pretending to gag. "And I don't want to be in band. I only have time to practice one thing, and that's snowboarding. And what'll the team think, anyhow?"

"It will be spit free, I'm sure." Grammy smiled. "And the snowboarding team will think you're multitalented, honey."

But Grammy was wrong. They'd think I was a traitor. And a geek.

The Band O' Geeks! And now I would be one of them. Nobody could ever find out.

## Chapter 2
# NOT FUNNY

**After supper, I headed across the street** and knocked on Yulia's door.

"What's up, Tally?" Yulia asked, letting me in.

"It's my grandparents." I flopped my head sideways and bugged my eyes out. "They've officially lost it. As in totally craze-o."

Yulia peeked through the blinds. "Everything looks normal over there to me. Except it's January, and your Christmas lights are still on."

"Things may look normal, but don't let them fool you." I peeked through the blinds, too, and then snapped them shut. "They're un-normal."

"It's abnormal."

"Right. Both." I nodded. "It's double bad. They're un-normal *and* abnormal."

"Are you okay?" Yulia asked.

I shook my head. "Can we talk?" I scanned the room. Yulia's dad was kicked back channel surfing, so I added, "Alone?"

"Sure, let's go to my room."

I followed Yulia down the hallway. Sheet music lay scattered across her bed. I plopped down and picked up a page. There were all sorts of lines, all filled with weird notes. Some were black. Some were open. A few had dots behind them. But none of them made any sense to me. I'd had the same problem with guitar until I learned to play by ear. "What language is this in?" I asked.

"Uh, music?" Yulia laughed. "That's the new song I told you about. I've almost got it."

"Can I hear it?"

Yulia's eyes widened a little. Probably because I'd never asked to hear any of her band songs before. But she grabbed her case, put her clarinet together, and started playing. Yulia's fingers danced over the keys. It was sort of pretty to watch. But the keys looked delicate, moving up and down beneath her fingertips. Clarinet took a gentle touch.

Delicate and gentle—I wasn't used to being either of those things. Snowboarding can be rough. I'd kill a band instrument. What were my grandparents thinking? I mean, seriously.

"How'd you like it?" Yulia asked as she finished.

I hugged my knees to my chest. "It's terrible," I finally said.

Yulia set her clarinet on her lap. "That's sort of mean."

"No, not you, Yulia! Your song was great. You don't even sound like you just joined band this year," I added quickly. "I meant my life is terrible."

"Okay, you're acting really weird tonight. Tell me what's going on already."

"Well, I don't want anybody to know. But I should tell you, I guess. You'll find out anyway when I show up at practice."

"Practice?" Yulia looked confused. "What practice?"

"Band practice." I took a deep breath. "My grandparents just told me they talked to Mr. Byrd and signed me up for band."

"You? In band?" Yulia laughed.

"I know, right? It's ridiculous."

I was glad Yulia agreed with me. At least someone besides me got that my grandparents had made a huge mistake. But I didn't like it when Yulia kept laughing.

"Hey," I frowned, "it's not *that* funny."

"Sorry," Yulia said, catching her breath. "I'm not laughing at you, Tally. I promise. But you always call us the Band O' Geeks. And now you're one of us?" She grinned. "That's pretty funny."

"Yeah, I guess so." I smiled. "Picture me hanging out with Sherman Frye, the band geek king."

Yulia shook her head. "Or Hope James."

"Or Baylor Meece!"

When they're not playing in band, she and Hope just sit around talking about band. I sighed.

"Don't forget Zac Wiles," Yulia said. "I can't see you hanging out with him either."

"Are you kidding? I can totally see myself hanging out with Zac."

Yulia looked at me like I *must* be joking. "Really?"

"Really." I nodded. "Hello! Zac is super cute."

"He is cute," Yulia agreed. "But he always wears camouflage. And he's always goofing off."

"That's part of what makes him cute, though."
But Yulia was right. Zac is a major class clown.

"Isn't Jasper Fava in band, too? He has the best
eyes," I said all dreamily. "They're like a bright blue
sky the morning after a snowfall."

"Come back down here out of those clouds."
Yulia snapped her fingers in front of my face.
"Besides, all the girls like Jasper."

Yulia and I didn't say anything for a few minutes.
My brain was still processing the fact that I was now
in the Band O' Geeks, just like all of the other geek
kids we'd just talked about. But I knew I wouldn't
fit in.

I shivered. "Yulia, I can't do it. I mean, look at
me. Do I look like a band geek to you?"

She looked me up and down, from my snow
boots to my fuchsia hat and gloves. "Nope. You
don't look geeky to me," Yulia finally said.

"Thank you! And besides," I went on, "I hardly
even know what a French horn is."

"It's a brass instrument. And it has like twelve feet of tubing," Yulia explained. "The tubing is all coiled up. And I think you'll like the way it sounds," she added. "It's warm and rich and velvety."

"Warm isn't good for park rats," I said. "And the snowboarding team can't ever find out about band. Ever."

Yulia shrugged. "What's the big deal?"

"The big deal is they'd never understand. So it's not happening!"

"So how are you going to keep band a secret, Tally?"

"I haven't figured that part out yet. But since Zoe Yates and Carsyn Casey are both on the team *and* go to our school, I have to come up with something. Fast."

"I have an idea." Yulia smiled. "C'mon."

So I followed Yulia downstairs.

# Chapter 3

# ALL HAIL THE SNOWBOARD QUEEN

**In the basement, Yulia flicked the light** switch. "Ta-da!"

"I get it! I'll hide out in your basement!" I nodded, checking out my new space. "But don't forget to bring my breakfast down here in the morning."

"No!" Yulia laughed. "I meant this." She nudged a huge trunk labeled Costumes. "See? If you wear a disguise, Zoe and Carsyn won't know it's you going into the band room."

"That's not a bad idea either. But," I eyed the Foosball and Ping-Pong tables on the other side of the room, "I think I'd like living down here."

"Nah, your grandparents might notice if you didn't come home for, like, a year." Yulia said. Then she opened the trunk. "Check out these costumes."

"Wow! Yulia!" I ran my fingers over a buttery yellow beaded dress that looked like something out of a glamorous Hollywood movie. "Beautiful!"

"Yep." Yulia pulled it out. "And there's more."

Underneath the dress was a poodle skirt and saddle shoes. Then there were some funny costumes like a chicken, a hot dog, and an octopus. And underneath those were tons more.

"Where'd you get all of this stuff?" I asked, digging through a bunch of crazy wigs.

"You know my dad's a car salesman."

"Yep," I said, pulling on a braided wig.

"He gets some cars from auctions. And a couple of months ago this guy Jimmy was at an auction, too. He was closing his costume shop, and he talked Dad into buying all of this. Isn't it great?"

"It is," I agreed, swapping my blonde braids for electric blue curls. "How do I look?"

Yulia looked up. "Perfect! I'd never guess it's you under there."

I headed over to see my new do in a full-length mirror hanging on a wall. Then I wound a curl around one finger, stretched it out, and let it spring back into place. "There's only one problem."

"What?" Yulia asked.

"If I don't want Zoe and Carsyn to know it's me, do I really want them to notice me? I mean, everyone'll probably want to know who the girl with the blue hair is."

"True." Yulia dug through the trunk again. "So I'm guessing a mermaid is out?" She dragged out a long tail covered in shiny purple scales. "Too bad, too. Mr. Byrd would probably love this as much as he loves the beach."

"Yeah, what's up with that?" I asked. "It's like twenty degrees outside, and he's walking around school in flip-flops, shorts, and tropical shirts."

"He just likes them, I guess." Yulia shrugged. "But Zac always jokes that Mr. Byrd's too cheap to fly south for a vacation. Get it?"

"Yeah, Byrd and fly south. I get it." I smiled.

"So," Yulia continued, "Zac lives near Mr. Byrd. And he said Mr. Byrd bought an aboveground pool, a beach umbrella, and a tiny palm tree in a flowerpot. And that he calls it his Backyard Oasis."

I laughed at first. But then I remembered what some kids said about him. "I heard Mr. Byrd's like a drill sergeant in the band room."

"Only sometimes. He just really loves music. And he was a band geek," Yulia explained. "He knows his stuff, and he wants us to know ours, too."

I didn't say anything.

"Don't worry, you'll like him. At first I wasn't sure either, but now he's my favorite teacher."

"Cool," I said. But really, it didn't matter if I liked Mr. Byrd or not. All that mattered right now was keeping the snowboarding team from finding out about me being in band.

So we rummaged through the trunk some more. And Yulia and I tried on different outfits, sort of like our own costume fashion show. I was a cowgirl. Yulia was a ninja. Then she changed into a princess dress, and I tried on a pirate costume.

"Yo-ho, me Band O' Geek mateys," I practiced my best growly pirate voice for band tomorrow. "If the team finds out I'm here, they'll make me walk the plank. And shark bait I will be. Arrr!"

"Love it!" Yulia laughed while I waved around a plastic sword.

"Nah, the eye patch is too creepy," I decided. "Maybe we can find something a little less weird."

"Like this outfit from the movie *Grease*?"

"Hey, those dark glasses are perfect, Yulia!" I slipped them on and then blew kisses to myself in the mirror. "But that pink jacket, not so much."

"Yeah, too bad it's not more like the jacket with the biker costume," Yulia said.

"I know." I frowned. But then I tried on the biker jacket with the pirate pants. "I got it, Yulia! I'll just mix and match!"

Yulia smiled. "That's a great idea."

So by the end of the night, I had *Grease* sunglasses, a biker jacket, striped pirate pants, and platform shoes from a groovy hippie costume. And instead of a wig, a green scarf from one of the costumes perfectly hid my short black hair.

I stared into the mirror. "You know, Yulia, I always wanted to start a new trend."

"It does look pretty good," Yulia agreed. "Like you should be a fashion model on some runway."

"Yeah, I like this new look," I said, propping the sunglasses on my head. "But tomorrow, we have to make sure Zoe and Carsyn don't find out it's really me going into the band room."

"Don't worry. I'll cover you," Yulia promised.

And the next day, Yulia did. I brought the costume in a duffel bag and changed into it right after lunch, just before band. While I waited in a bathroom stall, Yulia checked to make sure nobody was around.

"Psst, Tally!" Yulia whispered. "All clear!"

I eased open the door and followed Yulia into the hallway. We rounded the corner, and there they were. Zoe and Carsyn. We almost bumped right into them. I suddenly remembered they had PE after lunch. And the gym is right down the hall from the band room. I'd probably run into them here every day. Not good!

"Watch it, cool thing!" Zoe said, eyeing my sunglasses. I thought for half a second she was on to me. But then she went right on talking to Carsyn. They hurried into the gym while Yulia and I hurried into room 217, the band room.

Some kids were already warming up, so I sat in the back, hoping nobody would notice me. And besides, there was an empty chair right beside, *Squeal!*, Jasper Fava. He was twirling his drumsticks round and round his fingers.

"Rad outfit," Jasper said to me.

"Thanks! And your banana is really cool."

"My banana?" he asked.

*What a goof!* "I meant your bandana."

Jasper's thick black hair jutted around the American flag bandana he wore on his forehead. And mirrored sunglasses were clipped to the neck of his black T-shirt. Not everyone could pull off this sort of hippie style, but Jasper could.

"Gotcha." He smiled. "Thanks."

Suddenly I was too busy crushing on Jasper to be worried about band.

But then Yulia leaned in between us. "The percussionists sit here, Tally," she said. "And you should probably go get your French horn."

"Good idea," I said. "See ya, Jasper."

He smiled again. "For sure."

So I'd just slip on down to Mr. Byrd's desk to grab my French horn. No big deal.

Until Mr. Byrd made it one. "May I help you?" he asked.

"I'm Tally Nguyen," I whispered.

Mr. Byrd cupped one hand behind his ear. "Speak up, please," he said.

"I'm Tally Nguyen," I said a little louder.

"Oh, yes," Mr. Byrd said. "I spoke with your grandparents. Lovely people."

I wanted to say, *Usually, except when they signed me up for band.* But I just nodded instead.

Then Mr. Byrd made it an even bigger deal. "Class, kill the sound, please." He made a slashing motion. "I'd like for you to welcome our newest band member, Tally Nguyen." Then he reached behind his desk and set a case on top of it with a thud. "Tally, here's your instrument."

"Thanks," I said, grabbing the case. My case. I tried to hurry away, but Mr. Byrd stopped me.

"And Tally, is there a medical reason for your dark glasses?"

Trick question. Grammy told me that no one ever died of embarrassment. But if the snowboarding team found out my secret, I'd be the very first case of death by embarrassment. So technically, yeah, I did need them for a medical reason—life or death.

"Unless the answer is yes, please remove them," Mr. Byrd continued. "How do you expect to read your music?"

I looked at Yulia. She and everybody else in the room watched like they were glued to a video that just went viral. Since I didn't have a doctor's excuse, I had no choice. I plunked my glasses into the pocket of my biker jacket.

"Thank you," Mr. Byrd said. "Now, you'll be sitting with the other French horns in the brass section. Lucas, please raise your hand so Tally will know where to sit."

All I had to look for was the band geek waving his hands like he was flagging a plane.

"Did you hit a tree on your snowboard and get amnesia, or something? This is the band room. B-A-N-D," Zac Wiles said as I shuffled past.

"Nice one," I said, not letting the laughs from Zac's joke bother me as I squeezed past some trombonists with my super-sized case.

"Look out!" Kori Neal said, hugging her trombone close to her chest.

"No, snowboarders don't look out. They wipe out," Jack Cassilly III added. "And so does that outfit. Who dresses like that?"

That got more laughs. But I didn't let Jack get to me either. He can be a real jerk sometimes. Everyone says it's because his parents are loaded.

"Hey, I like this outfit. And I don't wipe out," I said. "I'm the Snowboard Queen." And that was true. That's what all of my teammates call me. But as soon as I said it, I wished I hadn't.

Because then, Zac said, "Did you hear that? The Snowboard Queen is gracing the lowly band room with her royal heinie." He made a big show of holding on to the saxophone attached to the strap around his neck and bowing to me.

"All hail the Snowboard Queen!" Jack laughed.

Okay, so I didn't expect them to tease me about snowboarding. But I was in Band O' Geeks territory now. And they could tell all of the lame jock jokes they wanted. I got it.

And I also got where I was supposed to sit. "You can stop waving your arms already," I said, plopping down beside Lucas.

"Welcome to band." Lucas smiled, flashing his braces. "But jocks aren't usually in band."

"Why, is there a law against it?" I halfway hoped there was.

"Nope." Lucas shook his head and smiled again. "I just didn't think you'd, you know, have time for something this, well, time-consuming. Plus, split loyalties and all that," he added.

"Of course I can handle both." I sat up a little straighter. "And I'm slightly offended, too. But, um, if you can show me how to put this thing together, I'll get over it," I said, unlatching my case.

So Lucas helped me twist the mouthpiece into what he called the leadpipe. After that, band got a little easier.

Mr. Byrd led everyone else through some exercises. And then while they ran through their songs for the upcoming dance, he came over and helped me with my French horn. I had a lot of catching up to do. He showed me how to buzz into the mouthpiece. And he showed me how to hold my new instrument with my left-hand fingers on the valves. My right hand rested inside the bell.

At the end of class, Mr. Byrd gave me some sheet music to take home to practice. And he said, "We don't usually have many kids sign up to play French horn, Tally. So we're glad to have you."

Except I wasn't the one who signed me up. That was Grammy and Pop. Still, I said, "Thanks."

I was also thankful the jokes died off as practice went along. But as I was putting my horn back into its case, I heard Jack say, "Who does Tally think she is, signing up for band second semester? The rest of us have been practicing all year. At least."

"She's the queen, remember?" Zac perched a pretend crown on his head. Some people laughed.

I wadded my sheet music into a tight ball and shoved it in my pocket. Then I stormed past them. Who needed the Band O' Geeks? In a little while, I'd be at snowboarding practice where I belonged.

# Chapter 4

# HERE'S THE DEAL

**As soon as we pulled out of the** school parking lot that afternoon, heading to practice, Grammy asked, "How was band today?"

"Terrible." I leaned back against the headrest. "The band room is no place for a snowboarder."

Grammy frowned. "What does snowboarding have to do with playing an instrument?"

"Everything," I sighed.

"Don't you think you're being a tiny bit dramatic, Tally?"

I shook my head. "Nope. I don't fit in with the band kids, Grammy."

"I remember when you said the same thing about the snowboarding team the first week you started," Grammy said, switching lanes. "Do you?"

"Maybe." I didn't want to admit it, but Grammy was right. I did say that when I first started snowboarding lessons.

"Maybe?" Grammy's mouth dropped open. "I remember after your first practice you said you'd never go back."

So that thing about old people being forgetful? That's a big fat lie. Grammy never forgets anything.

"But you did go back. And you've loved it ever since," Grammy continued.

She was right about that, too. I really do love snowboarding. But I'd never love band. And that's exactly what I told her. "See? That's different. Snowboarding is fun. Band isn't. I'll never love it. Or like it, even."

Grammy smiled. "We'll see."

"So what if I don't?"

"But what if you do?" Then her smile got even bigger. "What if you love being in the Band O' Geeks, as you call them?"

"Me? Love being a band geek?" I laughed. "Not happening!"

"I hope it does," Grammy said. "Not only does playing an instrument give you talent, it also teaches values and work ethic. That's why Pop and I signed you up for band."

This whole conversation sounded like "blah, blah, blah, blah, band" to me.

But then I thought about some of the other classes Grammy and Pop signed me up for: braiding rugs, painting self-portraits, and dehydrating fruits and vegetables. After a couple of months, those classes were over. The end.

But band classes were different. They never ended. They went on and on and on. Forever. So what if Grammy and Pop made me stick with band for the rest of my life? I couldn't let that happen.

I had to do something about this. Right here. Right now. Before things went too far. "So here's the deal, Grammy," I said.

"What deal?" she asked, turning onto Peligran Lane. We were almost to the chalet.

"So if I love band, I'll just keep playing, right?" I said. "Simple."

Grammy nodded. "It is to me."

"But if I don't love band, I get to quit."

Grammy frowned.

"And I'll do something else instead of band," I quickly added.

"Like what?"

"Like—" I paused. "Dunno. I haven't gotten that far yet."

Now Grammy laughed as she turned off the car. "Let me know when you think of something. But," she added, "it has to be an activity that's just as meaningful as band."

"Deal," I said, holding out my hand.

Grammy dropped her keys in her purse. "Deal." She shook my hand. "But I wouldn't think too hard about choosing another activity."

"Why?" I asked.

"Because you're going to love band. Just wait."

She was so wrong. But I didn't have time to tell her that. I had to meet the snowboarding team by the chalet at the bottom of the hill, like usual. We practice at a big resort. And before we ever hit the slopes, we always begin with warm-ups.

As soon as I walked in, Zoe and Carsyn smiled and waved. I was pretty sure they weren't on to me about band. My disguise had worked today. So all I had to do was keep wearing it, and they'd never catch me going into the band room.

Plus, with Zoe and Carsyn, if you didn't shred snow, you didn't exist. So they'd never talk to the band geeks. And everyone else went to different schools, so my secret was safe. Probably.

"Tally!" Coach Porter called. "Would you mind joining the team for warm-ups today?"

"Sorry!" I dropped my duffel bag on a bench and launched into stretches beside Addie Dillard.

"What's up with you?" Addie whispered.

"Uh, nothing." I sank into a squat. "Why?"

"Because you're nibbling your bottom lip like it's a hunk of cheese, which means you're nervous."

Addie and I became friends as soon as I joined the team. So she knows me pretty well. But still, I couldn't even tell Addie about band. It was too much. I tried to stop thinking about band and focus on what I really loved: snowboarding.

"I'm okay." I smiled at Addie. "I promise."

"I hope so. Moonlight Shred is only four days away."

"I can't wait," I said, moving on to lunges. Moonlight Shred is super fun. It's at night, and it's like everything disappears into the darkness. Everything except the slope since it's all lit up. It's our first big competition of the season.

"You're the best snowboarder on our team. I think you have a real shot at beating Gemma," Addie said.

"I don't know. Gemma's so good." Gemma Festen is on another snowboarding team. And she is serious competition. Last year at every competition, first place always went to either Gemma or me. That's why the team nicknamed me the Snowboard Queen.

"So are you." Addie smiled.

I hoped so. I hoped I was even better than last year. I'd spent hours on the rails, nailing my tricks.

Finally, Coach said, "Gear up! Meet me in five!"

Addie and I raced to the locker room with the rest of the team to change into layers of long underwear, snow pants, and our team jackets.

"Your jacket looks great on you, Tally. That's your color," Addie said.

"Thanks!" I zipped it up. This year's jackets were icy blue with dark gray stripes, a major improvement over last year's barf yellow and green.

Coach Porter waited for us by the chalet door, and we followed him outside and over to the ski lift that took us to the top of Peligran Peaks.

After I kicked all thoughts of band right out of my head, the rest of practice was as smooth as the icicles glittering on the pine trees in the distance.

"Good job stomping those tricks out there, Tally," Coach said as we headed back to the chalet.

"Thanks!" I said.

But was I good enough to beat Gemma? I'd find out on Saturday.

# Chapter 5

# CLOSE CALL

**By Friday, I was so good at changing** from my regular clothes into my band disguise, it only took me two minutes and thirty-nine seconds. Yulia timed me. But I wanted to get faster. Under two minutes was my goal. So today, I decided I wouldn't even hide in a stall while I changed.

"Are you sure?" Yulia looked sort of worried.

And then I heard this "purrrrr-rup" sound.

"Whoa, Yulia, your stomach!"

"Yeah, I guess today it's a purring kitten?"

When Yulia gets super nervous, her stomach makes funny sounds. Like a rumbling train, a leaky basketball, or burgers sizzling on a grill. It embarrasses Yulia, but everyone is pretty much used to it. And weirdly impressed by it.

"Never mind that now," Yulia said. "What if someone comes in?"

"Nobody has all week," I said, slipping into the biker jacket. "Just watch the door."

"Hurry!" Yulia leaned against the concrete wall, her eyes glued to the door.

And then it happened. I was tugging on the striped pirate pants when Zoe walked in. Carsyn was right behind her. So far, I'd only run into them once in the hallway all week. This was so not good. At all! I scrambled inside a stall, but the hinges snagged the side of my pants.

"What's up, Tally?" Zoe said. She headed toward me, her boots clippety-clopping across the tile floor.

I was so busted. "Um, not much."

She eyed my jacket and pants then. "You know," she said, popping a stick of gum in her mouth, "I saw somebody else wearing an outfit just like yours this week."

"No way!" I acted surprised.

"Hey, that reminds me," Zoe went on, "I found something of yours at the chalet a couple of days ago. But I forgot to give it to you."

"Great! I hope it's my favorite headband. I can't find that thing anywhere," I said, trying to act cool while still attempting to unhook my pants without Zoe and Carsyn noticing. But I was stuck to the door. Practically superglued.

"Nope, it's not your headband." Zoe reached into her purse. "It's this." She held up a crumpled piece of paper. It was the sheet music Mr. Byrd had given me at the very first band practice this week. It must've fallen out of my pocket at the chalet.

*Kertttchch.* I tore myself from the stall door then, totally ignoring the sound of ripping fabric. See? I'd learned something from the boys in PE. When they stink up the whole gym, nobody ever claims it. So if I didn't claim it, then that sound didn't come from my pants. Nuh-uh. Wasn't me.

I squinted at the sheet of paper Zoe still held in her hands. "That's not mine. But thanks, anyway." I grabbed at the paper.

But Zoe was faster than me. She flipped over the paper. "That's funny," she said. "It seems like it

must be yours. It has your name on the back and everything."

"Really?" I tried to smile. "That is funny. I didn't write my name on there." And that was totally true. I didn't.

"So why's your name written on band geek sheet music?" Zoe asked.

"Who knows? Maybe it's a joke." It sure felt like one. A great big joke on me, thanks to Grammy and Pop.

"Yeah, that's not even your handwriting, Tally," Yulia said, coming to my rescue.

And that was true, too. Mr. Byrd must've written my name on there before he gave it to me.

I grabbed the sheet music then and wadded it up for a second time. "Who needs this? Not me," I said, tossing it in the trash.

Maybe Zoe and Carsyn would go away now. I mean, I liked them and everything. They were super cool on the slopes. But to hang out with them, you had to be a snowboarder. And Yulia wasn't. So when she spoke up, it was like they noticed for the first time that she was even in the bathroom.

"Isn't she a band geek?" Zoe asked.

"Yep," Carsyn said.

"Don't you need to go practice or something?" Zoe said to Yulia. "Beat it." Then she looked at Carsyn and smiled. "Get it?"

Carsyn laughed. "Yeah. Beat it, band geek."

Yulia's face turned bright pink. But she didn't budge. Or even say anything.

I felt bad for Yulia. But I didn't say anything either. I couldn't. Zoe and Carsyn probably already knew something was up after finding the sheet music with my name on it. And if I stood up for Yulia, things would be even worse. For me, anyway. And with Moonlight Shred only a day away, I couldn't risk losing my focus.

But I did finally say, "I'm about to explode, so you might want to get out now while you still can."

Then I ran toward a stall, clutching my stomach and hoping my toxic explosion warning worked.

And it did. A few seconds later, Yulia said, "They're gone!"

So I ran back out. "Whew! That was super close. I thought they were on to me for a second."

"Me too. Are you okay?" Yulia asked. "I thought you were gonna explode."

"I'm fine," I said. "I meant I was about to explode all over Zoe and Carsyn if they didn't quit bugging you." I smiled. "But they didn't know that."

Yulia smiled, too. Then she started laughing.

"What's so funny?" I asked.

"You really shouldn't mix prints, Tally." Yulia pointed and giggled. "Flowers and stripes clash."

I looked down to see what Yulia was talking about. My pants! I'd almost forgotten they were ripped. And the hole was just big enough to flash my flowery undies. "Thanks!" I said, tying the biker jacket around my waist to hide them. I was going to need a new costume next week. People were probably starting to wonder, anyway!

"And thank you for taking care of Zoe and Carsyn a few minutes ago," Yulia said.

"It's no biggie." I shoved my feet into the platform shoes. "Let's get outta here."

But all the way to the band room, I wasn't really sure why Yulia thanked me. Using the "I'm gonna explode!" excuse suddenly felt like a cop out. But Yulia was my friend. And I was too chicken to say anything to Zoe and Carsyn about the way they were acting.

When we got to the band room, Yulia sat with the other clarinets. I waved at Jasper before heading to the French horn section.

"Make room for the Snow Cone Queen," Zac joked as I squeezed past.

"Get it right," Jack added. "She's the Ice Queen."

"Brrrr!" Zac fake shivered. And they both laughed.

I just rolled my eyes and grabbed a seat beside Lucas. He'd sort of been giving me a French horn crash course this week.

"Did you practice buzzing into your mouthpiece last night?" Lucas asked.

I knew there was something I forgot. But I was spending all of my time preparing for tomorrow's competition. Not blowing hot air into a horn.

"Honest answer?" I asked.

Lucas nodded. "Yep."

"I didn't. Sorry."

"You really need to practice. It's the only way you'll get better."

"But I don't care if I get better," I said.

Lucas's eyes got almost as big as Jasper's drums. "Well, only four of us play French horn, so I care. A lot!" he said. "If you're playing badly, it affects the entire section. We all sound bad."

Whoa. Lucas really cared about this band stuff. "I'll practice right now," I said. And I buzzed my lips until they were numb. I couldn't even feel the mouthpiece against them anymore.

By then, Mr. Byrd was standing on the podium at the front of the room. Today, he wore khaki shorts paired with flip-flops and a colorful sea horse tropical shirt. He signaled for quiet.

"First chairs, please work with your section," he said. And just like every day this week, he came over to give me a little one-on-one help since I was the only band member starting midyear.

As Mr. Byrd walked past the saxophones, Zac said, "Mr. Byrd, you'll never believe this! I forgot my neck strap."

"Again?" Mr. Byrd sighed. "Get the hall pass, Zac. You know where it is."

He should. This was only my first week in band, but I had already figured out that Zac forgets something every single day. On purpose, I bet.

"Okay, Tally." Mr. Byrd stood in front of me now, with a blue folder tucked under his armpit. "How goes it with the French horn? Been practicing?"

"Sorry." I shook my head. "I have a really important snowboarding competition tomorrow, so I've been busy getting ready for that."

Mr. Byrd pushed his glasses up on his nose. "It sounds really important. But band is important, too. If you don't practice, you don't improve. Simple."

Lucas shuffled in his seat. When I glanced his way, he mouthed "Told you so!"

I got it. Band is important to some people, like Lucas. And Yulia. And Sherman Frye. Every day, he jogs around the band room and even does jumping jacks and stretches to warm up before he ever pops open his flute case.

But the difference is this. They're all band geeks. Band geekiness is, like, in their blood or something. And even if I wanted it to be, which I didn't, band just wasn't in my blood. Snowboarding was.

Mr. Byrd still looked down at me, like he was waiting for me to say something.

"I'll try to make more time for band." Hey, I said I'd *try*. That didn't mean I *would*.

But it satisfied Mr. Byrd. "Good. Please do," he said. Then he handed me the folder. "I'd like for you to complete these worksheets during our practice today."

I opened it up. He had to be kidding. That thing was stuffed with sheets. I was supposed to name the notes on the lines and spaces. Then I had to draw some of my own, plus those funny-looking treble clef thingies. "But I don't have anything to write with," I said.

He pulled a pencil from behind his ear and handed it to me. "You do now. Return it after class."

"Thanks," I said. *For giving me a ton of work.*

Mr. Byrd hopped back on the podium. "Let's run through the songs for the dance. Play like the musicians you are!"

So while they ran through their dance songs, I ran through worksheet after worksheet until my hand cramped up. I was so glad when Mr. Byrd told everyone to put away their instruments.

But then Mr. Byrd made an announcement that changed my life. "I have something to share with you all," he began. "It's important to support each other, both inside and outside of this band room. So if any of you can, head out to Peligran Peaks tomorrow to support Tally Nguyen in her snowboarding competition. What time is it, Tally?"

"Five o'clock," I said so low I could barely hear myself.

Mr. Byrd cupped one hand behind his ear. "What's that?"

"Five o'clock," I said a little louder.

"Did you hear that, everyone? The competition is at five o'clock tomorrow evening. I'm sure she would appreciate seeing you all there." Mr. Byrd smiled.

*No, she wouldn't appreciate it. At all!* I wanted to scream.

"I'll be there, rooting for my fellow bandmate. Go, Tally!" Sherman cheered, his brown curls bobbing up and down.

"You really don't have to come." I forced a smile. "I understand if you're busy."

"Nope," Sherman said. "I'm not busy."

Of course he wasn't. It wasn't like Sherman had a real life outside of this band room. What was I thinking?

And what was Mr. Byrd thinking, inviting the whole band? If they showed up and the snowboarding team found out, I was doomed. Zoe and Carsyn would think I was a total geek. And Addie would never think I could focus on snowboarding with all this going on.

I'd never been hurt on the slopes. Ever. But this seemed like the perfect time to fake a broken something. An arm. A leg. A rib would do.

## Chapter 6
# MAKE A WAVE

**"Great run, Tally!"** Coach Porter gave me a gloved thumbs-up at the bottom of Peligran Peaks the next day.

"Thanks!" I said, high-fiving Addie, Zoe, and Carsyn.

"I'm proud of you girls. All of you," Coach added.

We'd just completed the semifinals of our snowboarding competition. Everybody got two rides down the hill. Whoever got the highest scores moved on to the next round. Carsyn was the only one of us who didn't make it through to the finals.

"I'm sorry, Carsyn," I said. "Seriously, you were *so* close."

Carsyn tugged off her helmet. "Yeah, maybe next time. But I hope one of you wins."

"Me too," Zoe said. "I'm gonna stomp some tricks *and* the competition."

"I like your enthusiasm, Zoe, but don't get too confident," Coach said. "It could kill your run."

Zoe shrugged. Then something on the sidelines caught her attention. She pointed and said, "Hey, Tally! Aren't those your grandparents?"

I glanced over. "Yep."

Grammy and Pop were doing the wave. No kidding. So that was bad enough. But even worse, the Band O' Geeks had showed up. Yulia, Sherman, and even Jasper were there, all doing the wave, too. And Baylor Meece was with them.

Besides playing clarinet in band, Baylor is a reporter for the *Benton Bluff Bloodhound*, our school paper. Beside her was some other kid I didn't recognize. Was he with them? Or did they just recruit him to do the wave, too?

"Why is that boy on the end holding up, like, a clarinet case?" Carsyn asked.

That was Sherman. And when he saw us looking his way, he waved his flute case even higher.

"Who knows? Probably some crazy kid," I said.

But then Sherman started chanting my name, "Tally! Tally! Tally!"

"Apparently that crazy kid knows you, Tally. I've seen him before. He's a band geek. Sheldon, or something," Zoe said.

"That other girl is in band, too," Carsyn added. "She's the one who was in the bathroom with Tally yesterday."

"Wait a minute! They're all band geeks," Zoe said. "And now Sherwin is putting together his flute." She and Carsyn both turned to look at me.

"What's up with that?" Carsyn asked.

Zoe lifted up her goggles to get a better look at me. "Yeah, what's the deal here? First there was the sheet music I found with your name on it, and now this." She frowned.

This could not be happening.

"Do you know them, Tally?" Addie asked.

That was a trick question. "Sort of," I squeaked.

Addie looked confused.

"Well," I began, "you've heard all about my friend Yulia. That's her wearing the yellow earmuffs."

"Oh, right. I'd love to meet her," Addie said, heading over there.

"Wait!" I grabbed her arm. But maybe Addie wasn't like Zoe and Carsyn. Maybe she'd think the band geeks really were okay. But I didn't want to go over there. Not yet, anyway. "Let's wait until after the meet."

"Let's head back up, everyone. Finals, here we come!" Coach said then.

So I was saved by the ski lift. For now. But I couldn't stay on top of the hill forever. Eventually, I had to come back down.

I took one last look at the Band O' Geeks. By then, Sherman's flute was together. He blew into it, playing a song. I couldn't hear it above the crowd.

But it must've been good because Pop twirled Grammy around, right there in front of everybody. Unbelievable!

"Tally? Tally, are you coming?" Addie linked her arm through mine, tugging me toward the ski lift.

I nodded, pretending my stomach wasn't throwing down a few triple cork flips of its own. But I couldn't fool Addie.

"You're nervous, aren't you?" she asked on our way up the hill. "You're chewing your lip again."

I really was. But it wasn't because of going up against Gemma Festen for a medal. I wanted a spot on that podium. I wanted the top spot. And it wasn't because of performing in front of the huge crowd gathered on both sides of the course, either. I mean, both of those things were enough to make anybody nervous. But my stomach flipped and flopped because of the Band O' Geeks.

I almost fessed up to Addie. My mouth was open and everything. I wasn't the one who signed up for band! Grammy and Pop forced me to! I could tell Addie all of that. She'd get it, wouldn't she?

But instead of spilling my band geek guts, I just said, "I'll be okay."

By the time we made it to the tent where we'd hang out until it was our turn to ride, I seriously felt better. I remembered I was here for one reason, and that was to throw down my best tricks out there on the hill tonight.

"There's Gemma," Addie whispered.

Gemma walked past us with some of the girls on her team who had also made it through to the finals. Gemma shot me a look that was colder than the winds rattling the tent.

But I didn't let Gemma rattle me. I smiled at her. I bet that surprised her because then her eyes narrowed even more, sort of like a lazy cat.

Even Addie noticed. "Hiss!" She pawed at the air and laughed. "Gemma's got her claws out for you, Tally!"

But I was glad she did. Because now I was totally focused on this competition. I hoped my best tricks would be good enough to beat Gemma's. And I'd almost forgotten about the Band O' Geeks. Almost.

"While we're waiting on the judges to give us the go-ahead," Coach Porter said then, "let's do some light stretches to stay loose."

So we sort of huddled in a corner, stretching our hamstring and shoulder muscles until the first rider headed toward the gate. Addie would be the third rider down. I was number fifteen. And Gemma was sweet sixteen.

Each rider got to ride down twice in the finals. The judges would score us on creativity, technical difficulty, and style. Only the highest score of the two runs counted. Whoever had the highest points at the end of the night won first place.

When it was my turn, I slid into position and adjusted my goggles. As soon as the flag waved, I was off. The silver rail in front of me shined in the glare of the lights on each side of the course. I hit the first rail. No problem. Then I hit two more and rode them all the way to the end. Easy.

Then came my first jump. I did a 540, grabbing the tail of my board. And I landed clean. Next, I grabbed the board between my feet for a switch stance backside 180. Another perfect landing! It was a great run.

I pumped my fists in the air to celebrate as I slid over to wait for my scores.

Addie came over and slung her arm over my shoulders. "Tally, that was amazing!"

"Thanks!" I grinned. "It felt amazing."

Addie smiled back. "That's why you're the Snowboard Queen."

My score lit up the scoreboard then.

The crowd booed.

"Only 87.25? Ouch," I said. "That feels low."

"It's okay. Everybody's scores have been so far," Addie said. "The judges are holding back on us."

Then we both looked up the hill. "Gemma's next," I said.

So Addie and I watched Gemma's run.

"Wow! She's catching huge air," I said. Gemma may be my competition, but I had to admit she is good. Super good.

"She's pretty awesome," Addie said.

And the judges agreed. She scored a point higher than me.

"At least you're in second place right now, Tally," Addie said.

"Yeah, it feels like last year all over again. I'm still number two."

"Don't say you're number two." Addie smiled. "It sounds funny," she said, crinkling up her nose.

"Ha!" She was right. So I said, "Okay, I'm still second."

"That's better. But don't worry," Addie went on. "The judges are just saving the bigger scores for the next round."

If I was going to beat Gemma, I needed a bigger score. So I hoped Addie was right.

"Tally! Tally! Tally!" It sounded like the entire Band O' Geeks was shouting my name now as Addie and I walked past the crowd and hopped on the ski lift for our last ride up the hill.

"Your fans are cheering you on again." Addie waved at them as we slowly left the ground, our legs dangling over the edge of the seat.

But I refused to look at the Band O' Geeks. Gemma was on the lift in front of us. I stared straight ahead at her hot pink helmet. If I was going to beat her, I had to stay focused on snowboarding, not band.

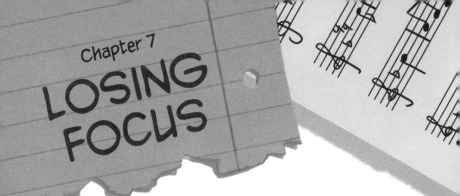

# Chapter 7

# LOSING FOCUS

"Don't worry about your scores on that run, Tally," Coach Porter said, right before I took my second ride down the hill. "Just dial in your timing. You'll wow those judges with your energy." He patted my shoulder. "Show 'em what you've got!"

I adjusted my goggles and took a couple of deep breaths.

"Ready?" the guy holding the flag asked.

I took one more big breath in and exhaled slowly through my mouth. Then I nodded. "Ready."

He waved the flag, and I slid down the hill. The first rail was in sight, and I locked on it. No problem. Neither were the next two rails. The top section was clean.

Then I had to throw down my first trick. I got both hands on my board for a double grab 540. I stomped the landing. After that, I went for a backside 720. I hadn't planned to. I'd only landed it a couple of times in practice. If I was going to beat Gemma, though, I had to just go for it.

But instead of eyeing the sweet spot for my landing, for a split second, I glanced at the crowd passing by in a blur of color. The Band O' Geeks was out there somewhere. And after this run, the entire snowboarding team would know the truth about me. *Tally Nguyen: Life of a Secret Band Geek.* It sounded like a movie title.

Taking my eyes off of the course was a big time rookie mistake. Seriously dumb. I mentally lost it. And then I lost my balance. I flailed my arms, trying to save the landing. But it was too late. Total wipeout! I slammed the ground. Hard.

I lay there on the snow for a minute, staring up at the lights overhead. From that angle, rings of light radiated away from them before disappearing into the night sky. It reminded me of the ripples skipping rocks make on a pond. It was sort of pretty.

Then there were more flashes of light. Photographers! I didn't want to make the front page of the local papers like this.

And I could just see Baylor's article for the *Bloodhound*, something like, "Snowboard Queen Wipes Out!" Just great. I pounded the snow with

mittened fists, unlatched one foot from my board, and tried to stand up. But I couldn't. At least, not very well.

"Ow! Ow!" I cried, limping around.

Then someone yelled, "She's hurt!"

Everything went all fast forward after that. The next thing I knew, I was lying on a stretcher. A guy wearing a bright red ski patrol jacket was staring down at me.

"My name's Larry, and I'm here to help you," he said. "Where's it hurt?"

"My left ankle," I said. "Is it broken?"

Then Coach Porter was there. So was Pop. And then I saw Grammy's worried face.

"Is my ankle broken?" I asked again.

But nobody answered me.

"Grammy," I tried again. "Is it?"

"Shh." She patted my cheeks, first one, then the other. "Just be still, Tally."

"Yep," Coach said. "Let him do his job."

"Ouch!" I almost came off the stretcher then. "That hurt!"

"I'm sorry," Larry, the ski patrol guy, began. "But there's good news. The ligaments in your ankle were probably just overstretched, causing a sprain."

"Are you sure? Because, trust me, it hurts like it's broken."

Larry smiled. "I know it hurts, hon. But you were able to stand a little on your own. And the pain seems more evident when I press on the tissues surrounding your ankle, and not the bone itself."

"So what's that mean?"

"It means," Larry said, placing an ice pack on my ankle, "that you'll need to follow the RICE guidelines. That means rest, ice, a compression bandage, and elevation."

"For how long?" I asked.

"At least for a couple of days. And you won't want to hit the slopes again for at least four weeks. Maybe six to avoid additional damage."

"No way!" Was he kidding? "Snowboarding season will practically be over by then."

"I'm sorry," Larry said. Then he looked at Grammy and Pop. "You may want to visit your family doctor tomorrow. Until then, give her over-the-counter meds as needed for pain relief."

"We will," Grammy said.

"And thank you," Pop added, shaking Larry's hand.

While Grammy, Pop, and Coach Porter talked to Larry, Addie came over to check on me. Zoe and Carsyn were right behind her.

"Tally! Are you okay?" Addie asked.

"Yeah, that fall did not look good," Zoe said.

Suddenly, Yulia and the rest of the band geeks were there, too. "I'm so sorry, Tally!" Yulia said.

"For sure," Jasper said. Then he smiled. "Man, that fall killed, but you're still a rad snowboarder."

"Thanks, Jasper." At least he didn't think I was a total goof after what happened.

"So are you going to be able to snowboard again?" Yulia asked.

I shook my head. "Larry there grounded me."

"Who's Larry?" Addie asked.

"Him." I nodded toward the ski patrol. "He said I sprained my ankle. I'm out for the season."

"Oh, no! I'm so sorry," Addie said.

Yulia patted my shoulder. "So am I."

"Me too," I said, eyeing the ice pack on my ankle. If it didn't hurt so bad, I'd kick the stretcher I was lying on. And maybe a few band geeks. Thanks to them, I'd lost my focus. And my shot at winning first place tonight. Or for the rest of the season.

Dumb band. Dumb Mr. Byrd for inviting the dumb band. And super dumb sprained ankle.

"So," Zoe began, frowning at the band geeks, "why are they all hanging out here, Tally?"

Now I had no choice. I had to come clean. Maybe with this sprained ankle, Zoe and Carsyn wouldn't pick on me about band. At least, not yet.

"I know you wondered that earlier, too," I began. "That's because my grandparents signed me up for band without telling me." I took a deep breath before rushing on. "So now I'm a band geek, too. But Grammy said I only have to do it until the end of this semester if I don't like it."

"Whoa," Addie said. "So is this Yulia?"

"Yep." I pointed to everyone else. "And that's Jasper, Baylor, and Sherman."

Jasper held up two fingers for the peace symbol. Baylor waved. Sherman said, "Greetings, snowboarders!"

I looked up to see what Addie, Zoe, and Carsyn would say. They all looked surprised, but none of them said anything. They didn't get a chance.

"Hey, aren't you going to introduce this band geek?" It was Zac's voice, but he didn't look like himself.

"Zac? I didn't even recognize you without your camouflage. Why are you dressed all in white?"

"Hey, if I wore green camouflage in the snow, I wouldn't be camouflaged, now would I?" He tapped the side of his head. "So I thought about it, and, duh, I changed my colors."

"Sort of like a chameleon, dude," Jasper said.

"Exactly!" Zac smiled. "My white clothes blend in with the snow."

"Leave it to Zac." Yulia laughed.

And I couldn't help it. I laughed, too. But then I wished I hadn't moved. "Ouch." I cringed. "My ankle really hurts."

"Hey, at least you're laughing," Zac said. "It beats crying."

"Yeah, I guess so. Cause that's what I feel like doing." I balled up a handful of snow and then flattened it. "What am I supposed to do for the next month and a half?"

"You still have band," Yulia reminded me. "Even with a bum ankle, you can play your French horn."

Oh, yay! Not. I forced myself not to roll my eyes.

"Yeah," Sherman chimed in. "And we'll come over to your house to cheer you up. I'll bring my yo-yo." When he isn't playing his flute, Sherman is always doing yo-yo tricks.

"We'll visit you, too," Addie said.

"I bet nobody'll cheer you up like your snowboarding team," Zoe added. Then she shot a look at the band geeks, like it was a cheer-up challenge to see who could cheer me up the most.

Zac crossed his arms. "You better look out, park rat! Tally will feel better in no time, thanks to us."

Whoa, that surprised me. Zac hadn't exactly welcomed me in the band room. I couldn't believe he even cared.

Then Jasper said, "Count me in, dudes."

I noticed something then. The snowboarders stood on one side of the stretcher. And the Band O' Geeks stood on the other. And I was stuck in the middle. It sort of felt like an omen, like eventually, I'd have to choose one side. Or the other.

# Chapter 8
# CHOOSING SIDES

**The next day, Grammy knocked on my** bedroom door. "Look who's here," she said.

I sat on my bed with my ankle propped up on pillows. I'd spent the last two hours twirling a red ribbon around and around my finger. It was the snowboarding medal I'd won last night. Second place. Again. Gemma won first place, of course.

"It's me!" Addie rushed in. "How's your ankle?"

"It's not as bad today," I said.

Addie set a plate of brownies on my nightstand. "I baked these myself."

"They look yummy." I smiled. "Thanks!"

"You're welcome. So, any chance you'll get to snowboard this season, after all?" Addie asked, sitting carefully at the foot of my bed.

"Not a chance," Grammy answered for me on her way out of my room.

I shook my head. "I saw my doctor this morning. She gave me crutches and said the same thing the ski patrol said last night. No snowboarding."

"That stinks," Addie said.

"Tell me about it."

"But at least you pulled out second place last night. What a way to go out, huh?" Addie grabbed my medal then, taking a closer look at it. "Nice," she said.

"Yeah, it is. And you know who else was nice?"

Addie shook her head.

"Gemma," I said. "She even told me she was sorry about my ankle."

"That was nice," Addie said, crossing her legs. "And Yulia seems nice, too. I thought she might be here."

"Me too. But I haven't seen her." *Or any of the other band geeks.*

"Knock, knock!" Grammy was at my door again. "More company!"

"Hey, Tally!" Zoe said. Carsyn was with her.

Zoe fist-bumped me and whistled. "Yikes! I still can't believe you're hurt."

"Yeah," Carsyn agreed. "You, like, never wipe out. You always land on your feet."

"So what happened, anyway?" Zoe asked, plopping down on a beanbag chair like it was story time at the library.

I shrugged. "I lost my concentration was all."

"You must've been daydreaming hard about the top of the podium," Carsyn said, eyeing my medal.

"Nah, that wasn't it," I said.

Zoe laughed. "Okay, then who is he?"

"Who's who?" I was confused.

"Your crush," Zoe joked. "Were you thinking of some guy instead of your landing?"

"No, there's no guy either."

Zoe folded her arms. "Seriously?"

"Well, I was thinking about Sherman," I said.

Zoe shot Carsyn a look and then said, "No way, Tally! You can't crush on a band geek."

"No!" I shook my head. "I wasn't thinking about him like that."

"Then how were you thinking about him?" Carsyn asked.

"The truth is, I was thinking about Sherman and the whole Band O' Geeks. I knew you'd find out after the competition about me being in band. And, well, I didn't want to be picked on like Creek the Band Geek."

"What?" Zoe said. "We wouldn't do that to you."

"Really? Not even one little joke?" I asked.

"Nope," Carsyn said.

This was weird. I couldn't believe they were totally fine with me being a band geek. Something was up. "What gives?" I finally said.

"You're not going to be a band geek for long. You said your grandma said you only have to finish out this semester in band if you don't like it, right?" Zoe said.

I nodded.

"Why wait?" Zoe stood up from the beanbag chair. "Say you don't like band. And then make sure nobody in the band likes you being in it, either."

"Huh?" Now this was getting way weirder.

"What Zoe means," Carsyn chimed in, "is we think you should just play really, really badly. Like terrible!"

"Then the band director will kick you right out," Zoe finished. "What do you think?"

I wasn't so sure about that. But I really didn't have time to think about it. Grammy was at the door again.

"Tally, you have more visitors," she said.

It was Yulia, Jasper, Sherman, Baylor, and Zac. Just like last night, they stood on one side of my bed. Addie, Zoe, and Carsyn were on the other side. And I was in the middle.

"Hi, Tally. We brought you something," Yulia said, holding up some paper.

"Look," Zac said, grabbing one end and pulling.

It was a giant banner with GET WELL TALLY in giant, lime-green letters.

"We wanted to come over sooner," Yulia said. "But we've been busy getting the whole band to sign this."

"Yo, even Mr. Byrd," said Jasper, pointing. Mr. Byrd had written *Practice!!!* along with a smiley face and his name. "Zac got that one, since he lives by Mr. Byrd."

"That's so cool," I said, reading all the names. "Seriously. Thanks, guys!"

"It was my idea," Sherman said.

Baylor nudged him. "That doesn't matter."

"Where do you want us to put it?" Yulia asked.

Jasper dug around in the backpack slung across his shoulder. "I brought tape so we could hang it."

I looked around my room, trying to find a spot where there wasn't a snowboarding poster. "Maybe above my closet. Then I can see it while I'm lying in bed."

Sherman went over and jumped up. "We can't reach it."

"Dude," Jasper slid out my desk chair, "I'll just stand on this."

So Zac held the chair steady while Jasper climbed up on it. Yulia handed Jasper the banner, and Baylor handed him pieces of tape.

"Wait," Sherman said. "It's crooked. Bring that end up more."

Jasper raised it up. "Better, man?"

Sherman cocked his head. "Now down."

Jasper lowered it. "Here?"

Sherman frowned. "Up just a touch."

Jasper raised it, like, half an inch. "Here?"

"Hmmm." Sherman eyed it again.

"You're taking too long, dude. It's going right here," Jasper said, sticking tape to the wall.

"Perfect!" Sherman said.

"Wow," Zoe said. "How many band geeks does it take to hang up a dumb sign, anyway?"

Carsyn smiled. "One, two, three, four, five. Five band geeks."

"Whatever," Jasper said, jumping off the chair. When he did, he bumped into my closet door and it swung open. He started to close it, but then he stopped. "Hey, that's one sweet guitar!" He pulled it out. "Do you play?"

Jasper and everybody else looked at me, waiting for an answer.

*Great.* "I used to play around on it some, but not so much anymore," I finally said. "I'm not that good."

"My uncle plays, and he taught me some stuff," Zac said then. "I mostly play by ear."

"Me too," I said. "All of the notes on the sheet music sort of scramble my brain."

Zac laughed. "Mine too. But don't worry. It gets better."

"I hope so," I said.

Nobody else seemed to notice the funny look Zoe shot me, like I was supposed to be getting out of this band stuff, not deeper into it.

"Mind if I play?" Zac asked, taking my guitar from Jasper.

"Sure, go ahead," I said.

So while Zac strummed a song, Jasper pulled drumsticks from his backpack. He beat a rhythm on the math book on my desk. Then a few chords later, Yulia started singing along. It sounded pretty good. When they finished, Sherman clapped. Baylor and I joined in, too. And even Addie. But not Carsyn. Or Zoe.

"Why don't you save it for karaoke night? Karaoke at the dog pound," Zoe joked. "Ah-rooo!" She howled.

"That's real funny," Zac said. "Not."

But Zoe was on a roll. "How are band geeks like a balloon?"

"How?" Carsyn asked.

"They're both full of hot air!" Zoe grinned.

"That was bad," Addie cringed.

"Yeah," Sherman said. "It stunk."

"Have you got anything better?" Zoe challenged.

"We came over to see Tally," Yulia said. "Not to be made fun of. She's our friend, too."

"You've seen her. So why don't you take your hot air out of here?" Zoe asked. "Tell them you pick us to stay and them to leave, Tally."

Yulia looked at me.

"Um," I began. And then I froze.

Baylor said, "Let's go."

"Gladly!" Zac leaned my guitar against my nightstand and followed Baylor out of my room.

Sherman, Jasper, and Yulia were right behind them.

A few minutes later, Grammy came in and shooed Addie, Zoe, and Carsyn out of my room, too. "You need your rest, Tally," she said when everybody was gone.

I tried to rest, but it was hard. Now the band geeks were probably all mad at me because I didn't stand up for them. And the snowboarders were probably mad because I didn't make the geeks leave in the first place.

And I was mad, too. At myself. Now that I'd calmed down, I knew it wasn't the band geeks' fault I wiped out on the hill last night. It was mine. I'm the one who took my eyes off the course.

Having to choose between my snowboarding friends and my band friends, if I could call them that, I mean, the snowboarders were my friends. But I'd been friends with Yulia for a long time. And some of the other band geeks were pretty cool, too. Who said I had to choose, anyway?

Then I noticed the guitar Zac left propped up by my bed. I scooted myself up, reached for it, and started to play. I got so into it I bobbed my head along. And I didn't even notice my bedroom door open.

"Righteous! You're playing your guitar!"

I stopped playing, suddenly embarrassed. "Jasper! What are you doing back?"

"I forgot my backpack," he said, reaching for it. "And I'm glad I did. You totally lied."

"About what?"

"You said you weren't good. But you are," he said. Then he snapped his fingers. "You should play at the school dance next weekend."

I saw my reflection in Jasper's sunglasses then. It was sort of a mix of surprise and fear. Me? Play at the dance? Nuh-uh. Not happening.

# Chapter 9

# THE COLD SHOULDER

On Monday, I hobbled on crutches into band practice.

"Hi, Baylor," I said.

Since Baylor was a school newspaper reporter, she usually talked a lot. But today, she didn't have much to say. Not to me, anyway.

"Oh. Hi." She sort of wrinkled up her nose and went back to looking at her clarinet reeds.

So I limped over to Yulia. "Thanks again for the banner yesterday. It looks great in my room."

Yulia glanced up from her sheet music just long enough to say, "No prob."

I spotted Sherman doing jumping jacks. "Hey, Sherman! I'm glad you came over yesterday."

He nodded, but he kept jumping and counting.

So I made my way to my seat. But where was Lucas? Then I noticed him talking to Mr. Byrd. Lucas said something, and Mr. Byrd shook his head. So Lucas turned around and headed over.

"Hi, Lucas. I practiced last night." Then I pointed at my crutches. "I have some extra time now."

"Good for you," Lucas said. Then he scooted his seat down as far as he could from mine. And I heard him whisper to the kid on his other side that he wanted to switch seats, but Mr. Byrd said no.

So Lucas was mad at me, too. And he wasn't even at my house yesterday! I guess Baylor, Zac, Sherman, Jasper, and Yulia told the rest of the band what happened. Now everyone was mad at me.

I hadn't been in band for long, but I'd started to like the band geeks. I mean, I was already friends with Yulia. But Baylor was really smart and nice, and Sherman had tons of energy. Jasper was fun. Zac made everybody laugh. And Lucas was like the French horn master. Zoe had made fun of them, but she was wrong. They were cool. And I was wrong not to tell her that before.

It's not like it mattered now, though. I'd blown it with the band. It was like being at Moonlight Shred all over again. Except this time, I'd wiped out in the band room. Totally messed things up. So how could I fix it? Could it even be fixed?

Mr. Byrd hopped on the podium then. "Let's bop the concert B-flat scale!"

Everyone started playing. Except me. I still didn't know anything about scales yet. So I just sat there while the band warmed up.

Then Mr. Byrd said, "The dance is Saturday, everyone. Today, I'd like for each section to play through the songs we'll be playing. If your section isn't playing, I want you to listen and offer feedback. But," he paused, "keep it positive. Encouraging suggestions only, okay? Trumpets, hit it!"

As the trumpets played, Mr. Byrd walked over to me. "I heard about Saturday. How's the ankle?"

At least Mr. Byrd was still talking to me. "It hurts, but it's getting better," I said.

"Wonderful," he said. "I sprained my ankle once. It was freshman year in high school marching band. The field was wet, and I slipped in the mud."

"That's right. Yulia told me you're an ex-band geek." *Oops.* Mr. Byrd might not like being called a geek. "Sorry. I mean, she said you were in band."

"That's okay. I don't mind being called a band geek. In fact," he smiled, "it's a privilege."

"Really?" I said.

Mr. Byrd nodded. "Really. I wasn't always a band geek, you know. Band takes everyone working together," Mr. Byrd went on. "At first, I was into surfing, so I didn't take band very seriously. The kids who did, well, they didn't like me very much."

I felt like that, like the whole band hated me.

"So what did you do?" I asked.

"Well, it was up to me to decide if band was important enough to really matter in my life. Once

I decided that it was, I stopped goofing off. When I practiced more, everything clicked." He smiled. "I became a real band geek. And I still am."

"What about surfing?" I asked.

Mr. Byrd laughed. "I'm no pro, but I still catch a wave every now and then."

Picturing Mr. Byrd on a surfboard made me laugh, too.

"And that's the really neat thing about life, Tally. It's okay to have lots of interests. And lots of different friends." He pointed to my French horn. "Are you interested in learning more about proper mouth placement for a correct embouchure today?"

I looked at my mouthpiece. My snowboarding teammates might not like it, but I said, "Yes, sir."

The trumpets finished playing, so Mr. Byrd told the saxophones to go next. Then he showed me how to set the corners of my mouth to focus the air inside my mouthpiece. And he told me not to puff out my cheeks. "Let's leave puffer fish in the sea."

"Okay." I puffed out my cheeks until they were the size of small balloons. Then I popped them with my fingers. "No puffer fish in the band room."

"Exactly!" Mr. Byrd smiled.

After all of the sections played through their dance songs, Mr. Byrd went back to the podium. "Now we're all going to play those songs together, everyone." He raised his arms, a baton in one hand, and counted, "One and two and ready and go."

I listened as the band practiced their songs together. Sherman's flute was light and airy, while Zac's saxophone was mellow. Baylor and Yulia's fingers flew over their clarinet keys. Then there was Lucas on his French horn, and the trombones, and the trumpets. And the beat of the drums kept them all in time. One person didn't make a band. It took everyone, all working and playing together.

It was different from snowboarding. Out on the hill, we're a team, but we stomp our own tricks. And we earn our own scores. I like it that way. But I also liked hearing all of the different instruments play together to make one big sound. I sort of wanted to be a part of that, too.

Before, I thought I could only snowboard. Or play in band. Not both. But Mr. Byrd was right. I didn't have to choose. Not between snowboarding and band. And not between snowboarders and band geeks.

But no one exactly wanted me in the band room right now. I mean, I totally deserved the cold shoulder. Music is important to them. And I'd acted like it was no big deal. I'd probably feel just like them if some new snowboarder didn't take our sport seriously.

Then there was what happened yesterday with Zoe and Carsyn at my house. I should've shut them down when they started cracking band jokes. But I didn't. And I couldn't go back and change it.

Just like I couldn't change that wipeout on the hill Saturday. But in snowboarding, when I wiped out before, I got up and rode the slopes again. Maybe with this band wipeout, I should try again, too, with what the Band O' Geeks loved most— music. It was worth a shot.

So as soon as band was over, I limped over to Jasper. He pulled a chair over for me. "Hi," I said.

"What's up, Snowboard Queen?"

"I feel more like the Queen of Crutches." I smiled sheepishly. "So, you're still talking to me?"

Jasper slid his drumsticks into his backpack. "Yo, I figure it's like this. You're in band now, too. Even if you don't want to be. So when you and your snowboarding friends make band geek jokes," he shrugged, "it's totally like you're making fun of yourself. Right?"

In a weird way, that sort of made sense. "I guess so," I said.

"So why would I be mad about you laughing at yourself?" He slung his backpack over one shoulder. "Wait a few days. They'll get over it."

"Maybe," I said. "A couple of days ago, I was mad, too. And now I'm not."

"What were you mad about?" Jasper asked.

"At first, I blamed you guys for my wipeout. I thought if you hadn't shown up at the competition, I would've stayed focused. And," I looked down, "there wouldn't be a bandage wrapped around my ankle right now."

Jasper nodded.

"After I calmed down, though, I knew I couldn't blame anybody but me. I took my eyes off the course." I sighed. "My new nickname should be the Snowboard Klutz."

"Nah, you're no klutz," he said. "And even if you were, you'd be a totally cute snowboarding klutz."

Whoa. Either I was hearing things because of some undiagnosed head injury from my accident, or Jasper Fava, one of the hottest band geeks, just called me totally cute. "Thanks." I smiled again. *Keep your cool, Tally.*

"Anyway, I'm the only one who can make things right with the band. With your help," I added.

"My help?" Jasper asked.

"Yep. But the dance is coming up fast."

Then I told him my plan. "So will you help me? Please? I know we don't have much time."

"For sure," Jasper said. "I'm super stoked. Everybody at the dance will love this."

And when Jasper said everybody, he meant everybody. Like, the whole school. This was either going to be amazing, or the wipeout of the century.

# Chapter 10

# FINDING MY WINGS

On Saturday, Grammy and I waited in the school parking lot. It was the night of the dance.

"Who's helping you get your things inside?" Grammy asked.

"Jasper," I said, hoping with each of the cars turning in that it would be him. He was already a few minutes late. And I was getting more nervous. What if Jasper didn't show up? What if our plan really did end up being a total wipeout?

But then Grammy took my mind off that when she pulled some brochures from her purse. "Take a look at these, Tally."

I flipped through them. Benton Bluff Nursing Center. Benton Bluff Library. Benton Bluff Animal Shelter. "What's all of this about?"

"Volunteer information, silly." Grammy smiled. "When we made our deal about you dropping band at the end of the semester, you said you didn't have any ideas for what you'd do instead. So I thought if band doesn't work out, you could give volunteering a whirl," she said all sing-songy.

"Oh, right. Thanks." I dropped them into my drawstring backpack. With everything that had happened since I sprained my ankle last week, I'd almost forgotten about that deal we'd made.

"Is that Jasper?" Grammy asked.

"Where?" Then I spotted him, too, heading toward our car.

Jasper had hung out at my house a lot this week to help with my plan, but I wasn't surprised Grammy didn't recognize him. He wore his usual bandana. But it was paired with a button-up shirt and dress pants.

"Yep, that's him." I swung open my door before I could chicken out on the dance. And our plan.

"He's handsome."

"Grammy!" I said. But she was right. I'd never seen Jasper look so, well, nice.

"Hi, Tally," Jasper said then. "Let me get your door."

"Thanks," I said.

"For sure." Jasper helped me with the door and my stuff.

Grammy looked at me and winked. "Polite, too."

I shook my head at her and sent a silent message from my brain to hers. *Please, don't embarrass me!*

But apparently Grammy wasn't receiving messages. She said, "Have fun dancing, you two." Then she pinched her nose with one hand and sort of waved the other hand around to do the swim dance move.

"Close the door quick," I said to Jasper.

He did, laughing. "Yo, your grandma's funny."

"Sometimes." *Just not so much when she's actually in public. Or around my friends.* "But it's a good thing that seat belt held her back. She'd have danced right into the gym."

And that's where Jasper and I were headed. Once we got to the hallway, I said, "Sorry you have to carry my stuff."

"No problem-o. It's not heavy. Not with these guns." Jasper nodded toward his muscles and smiled, wiggling his eyebrows.

I knew tons of girls liked him. But when Jasper smiled at me, it was like he only saw one girl. Me.

I smiled too, but I played it cool. "You have muscles? I hadn't noticed."

"Ha-ha. You better be glad you're on crutches." He held the gym door open for me then.

My heart beat even faster because of what we were about to do. But when I looked inside the gym, I almost forgot about being nervous. "Look, Jasper. It's beautiful!"

"Totally. Like an ice castle, or something." Jasper said.

The gym was dark, but blue uplights shined like icicles from the floor to the ceiling along every wall. White balloons floated above our heads like giant snowflakes. And silver tree branches, strung with clear lights, dotted the dance floor. Jasper was right. The gym really did look like an ice castle.

Music played from speakers set up onstage, but the dance floor was empty. Kids mostly sat at tables, topped with blue-and-white spreads.

"Tally!" Zoe waved. She sat at a table with Carsyn. And they'd gotten permission to invite Addie and a few of the other snowboarders.

"Hi, guys!" I said.

Addie hopped up and hugged me.

"I'm glad you're here," I said.

"Me too! But," she stuck out her bottom lip and made a sad face, "you're still on crutches."

"Only for another week," I said.

"It's just too bad you can't dance," Addie said.

"So far, nobody's dancing anyway."

"Yo," Jasper said. "We're totally gonna change that." He headed to the stage.

"Why is he carrying a guitar case?" Addie asked.

I shrugged. "Who knows?"

Even in the mostly-dark gym, I couldn't get anything past Addie. "Somehow, I think you know."

I just smiled.

"Sit with us, Tally!" Zoe yelled above the music.

"Not yet," I said. "First, I need to take care of something."

Then I followed Jasper to the stage, where all of the band instruments were already set up. He opened the guitar case. When I leaned my crutches against a chair and got my balance, Jasper handed my guitar to me.

I looked out at the crowd. I was more scared than I'd ever been in my life. "I'm not sure I can do this, Jasper. I've never played in front of anyone."

"You've played in front of me."

"Yeah," I pointed to the crowd, "but there are so many people out there." I mean, I was used to snowboarding in front of an audience, but this was totally different.

"And you've played in front of me, too," Yulia said, joining us onstage.

I'd already apologized to Yulia for everything that happened with Zoe and Carsyn and everyone at my house. So she'd been helping Jasper and me with our plan.

"You can do it." Yulia smiled.

"We love your playing. They totally will, too," Jasper said. "And you look great. So since you can't be on the dance floor, you need to be up onstage."

For some reason, Jasper's compliments embarrassed me even more than some of the stuff Grammy and Pop did. I was super glad it was dark. At least Jasper couldn't see my pink cheeks. They probably matched the tiny pink flowers on my skirt.

"Trust me," Jasper said. "You've got this."

Then I remembered why I wanted to do this in the first place. It was sort of an apology to the band geeks. And even though I loved snowboarding, I had to prove to myself that it was okay to do something else, too. That I wasn't boxed in.

"Let's do this," I said.

So Jasper gave Mr. Byrd a thumbs-up, and Mr. Byrd killed the music coming from the speakers. He was in on our plan, of course.

"Attention please, dudes and dudettes," Jasper said into the mic, before handing it to me.

I took a deep breath and spoke into it. "I hope everyone's having fun tonight. Everything looks amazing, right?"

There were some claps and cheers.

"So our seriously awesome school band is about to play for us. But before they come up onstage, Jasper, Yulia, and I have a song we'd like to play for you." I smiled then. "We wrote it ourselves. It's called 'Finding My Wings.'"

I slid the mic into the stand. Then Jasper started beating his drum, and I joined in, strumming my guitar.

After a few chords, Yulia's soft voice swept across the gym.

"Stars shine down, bright moonlight.

"I'm up here on this hill. Gonna prove myself tonight.

"But dreams, they fade. Away. Oh, away.

"Falling through the night sky, I found the nerve to say . . ."

Yulia paused while Jasper and I continued playing. Then her voice grew more powerful as she clapped and belted out the chorus.

"That I'm finding my wings. Yeah. Yeah. Finally finding me."

Yulia continued telling the story through song, all about feeling pulled in different directions.

That's when I noticed some kids hitting the dance floor. Sherman and Zoe were even dancing

together. Okay, maybe not exactly together. More like beside each other. But hey, it was a start.

And guess what else? Zoe wore red-and-white striped pants, sort of like the pirate costume I'd worn for my band disguise. Maybe I'd started a trend after all!

Near the end of our song, Yulia's voice and Jasper's drums faded, while I finished a riff. When we were done, the gym erupted in applause.

"Thank you!" Yulia said into the mic.

When the applause died down, I said, "That's a true story. I've been snowboarding for a couple of years, and I just joined band, too. I wasn't sure I could do both, but now I know I can." I scanned the crowd. "And I know I don't have to pick just one group of friends. I can hang out with the snowboarders *and* the band geeks."

I grabbed my crutches and limped over to a seat. I saw Addie, Zoe, and Carsyn smiling, and I knew everyone was going to be okay.

Finding my wings. That's definitely what I was learning to do. Being up onstage with Jasper and Yulia, I was sure of it.

Mr. Byrd grabbed the mic and said, "Thank you Jasper, Yulia, and Tally! Now let's hear it for our Benton Bluff Junior High band." The band came up onstage then.

"Hey, awesome job," Zac said as he walked by.

Mr. Byrd got up on the podium then and said, "I'm proud of you all!" Then he looked at me. "You shred snow *and* guitar. Well done!"

"And she's totally learning to shred the French horn," Jasper said.

"I'm not sure there is such a thing, Jasper. But maybe Tally just invented it." Mr. Byrd laughed. "Anyway, we're glad you're a band geek, Tally."

"Thanks, sir," I said. A band geek. That was me. So I wouldn't need Grammy's brochures after all. I was in band to stay. And now the whole world knew it, too.